Twenty-six Rabbits Run Riot

by Cara Lockhart Smith

Little, Brown and Company

Boston   Toronto   London

For my mother,
Margaret Lockhart Smith,
whose rabbits they were
in the first place

First U.S. edition

Library of Congress Catalog Card Number 90-52558

10 9 8 7 6 5 4 3 2 1

Published simultaneously in Canada
by Little, Brown & Company (Canada) Limited

Printed in Belgium

Who would have thought a nice person like
Mrs. Fitzwarren...

would have such naughty children? They rushed all over the house creating a shambles. Even the baby would not stay where he was put.

One sunny morning Mrs. Fitzwarren said,
"It's time for a nice day out. But the baby has
disappeared. Quick, everyone, look for that poor
little baby!"

So twenty-six rabbits searched and searched,
until at last they found the baby...

in the teapot!

Mrs. Fitzwarren wiped the tea off the baby and put him in his carriage. Then they all set out for the park. "Now run off and play," said Mrs. Fitzwarren, and twenty-six rabbits scattered in every direction. In a very short time they created absolute...

TO THE PARK

The park keeper shouted, "Take them away!" "Oh, I will," said Mrs. Fitzwarren, "but the baby's wriggled out of his carriage. Quick, everyone, look for that poor little baby!"

So twenty-six rabbits searched and searched, until at last they found the baby…

in the trash can!

Mrs. Fitzwarren brushed the trash off the baby and put him in his carriage. "Let's go have a picnic in the woods," said Mrs. Fitzwarren. Twenty-six rabbits rushed up the hill, and in less than a minute...

all the children disappeared!
　　(Where are they?)
　　Mrs. Fitzwarren blinked her eyes. Then she opened her mouth very wide and shouted:

RABBITS!

"Lunchtime!" Twenty-six rabbits came out of hiding and had an enormous picnic.

Mrs. Fitzwarren brushed the crumbs off the baby. "Let's go to the sea!" she said. They left the woods, crossed the dunes, and raced out onto the beach.

It was hot beside the sea. Mrs. Fitzwarren fell
sound asleep while her children made a castle in
the sand. Suddenly, Mrs. Fitzwarren woke up,
looked around, and cried, "Oh, where is that
baby? He's lost again! Quick, everyone, look for
that poor little baby!"

So twenty-six rabbits searched and searched,
until at last they found the baby...

in the castle!

Mrs. Fitzwarren shook the baby to get rid of the sand, and put him in his carriage. "I could do with a nice cup of tea!" she sighed. So off they went to a restaurant. "Twenty-six ice creams and one cup of tea," said Mrs. Fitzwarren.

Very soon, twenty-six rabbits caused quite an
uproar in the restaurant. "You've a very fine
family, but could you please take them home,"
said the owner to Mrs. Fitzwarren. "Oh, I will,"
she said, "just as soon as we find our baby.
Quick, everyone, look for that poor little baby!"
Twenty-six rabbits searched and searched,
until at last they found the baby…

nowhere!

"Oh!" wailed Mrs. Fitzwarren, "my poor little baby! I just can't go home without him!" She wept enormous tears; her face was all dripping. She burrowed around, looking for a handkerchief. "Oh," she said, "the baby is . . ."

in my handbag!

She kissed the baby all over and put him in his carriage. "Time to go home," she said. It was growing dark as they left the restaurant.

When they got back it was nighttime.

They had hot milk and cookies. Mrs.
Fitzwarren gave them all a good scrub (especially
the baby, who was filthy) and put them to bed.
Then she went downstairs and made a mug of
steaming hot chocolate.

"How peaceful it is," she sighed, sitting by the blazing fire. Little did she know!

For her children were not in their beds. Oh, no, on the contrary, they were all outside in the garden, gallivanting under the moon. Except for the baby...

who was fast asleep.